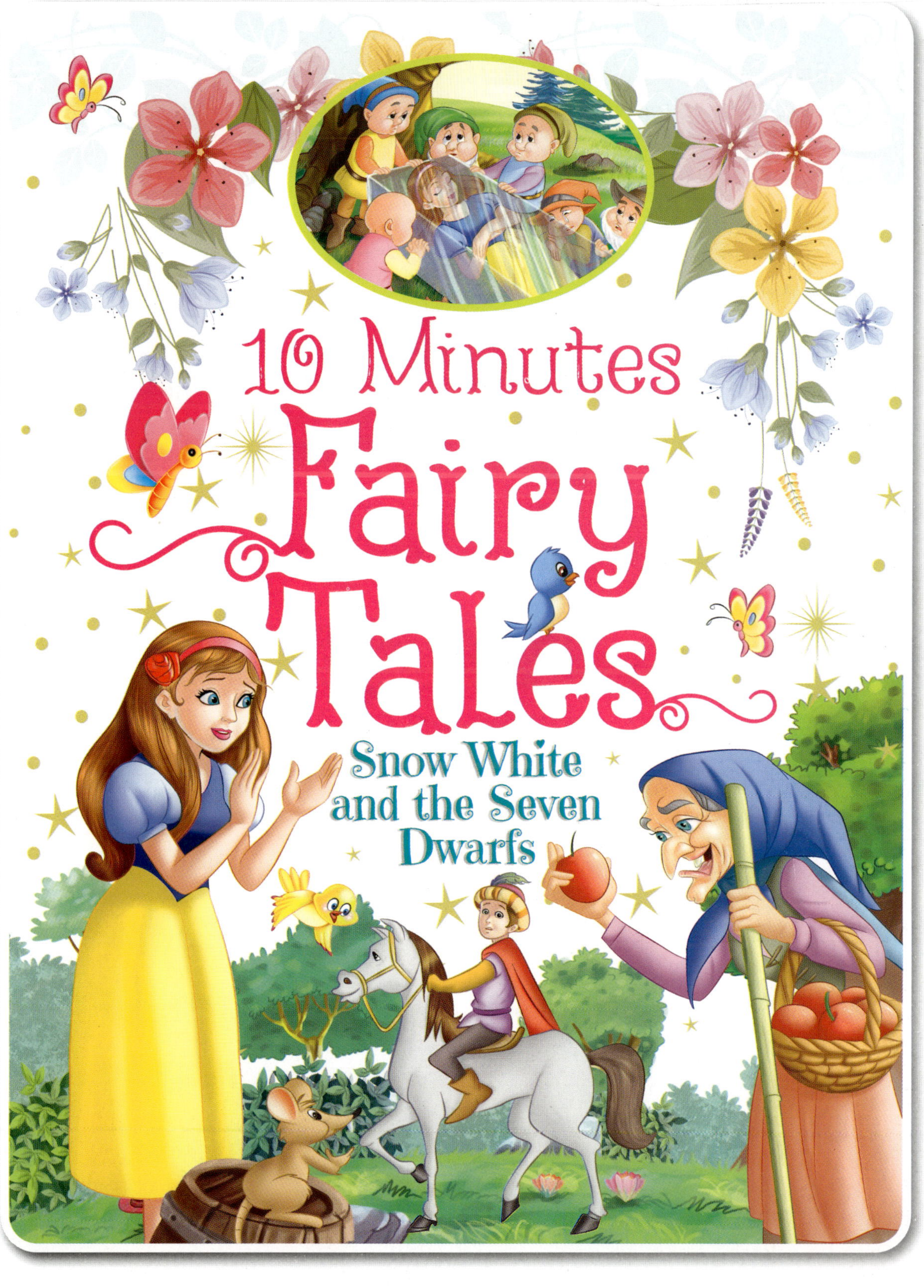
10 Minutes
Fairy Tales
Snow White and the Seven Dwarfs

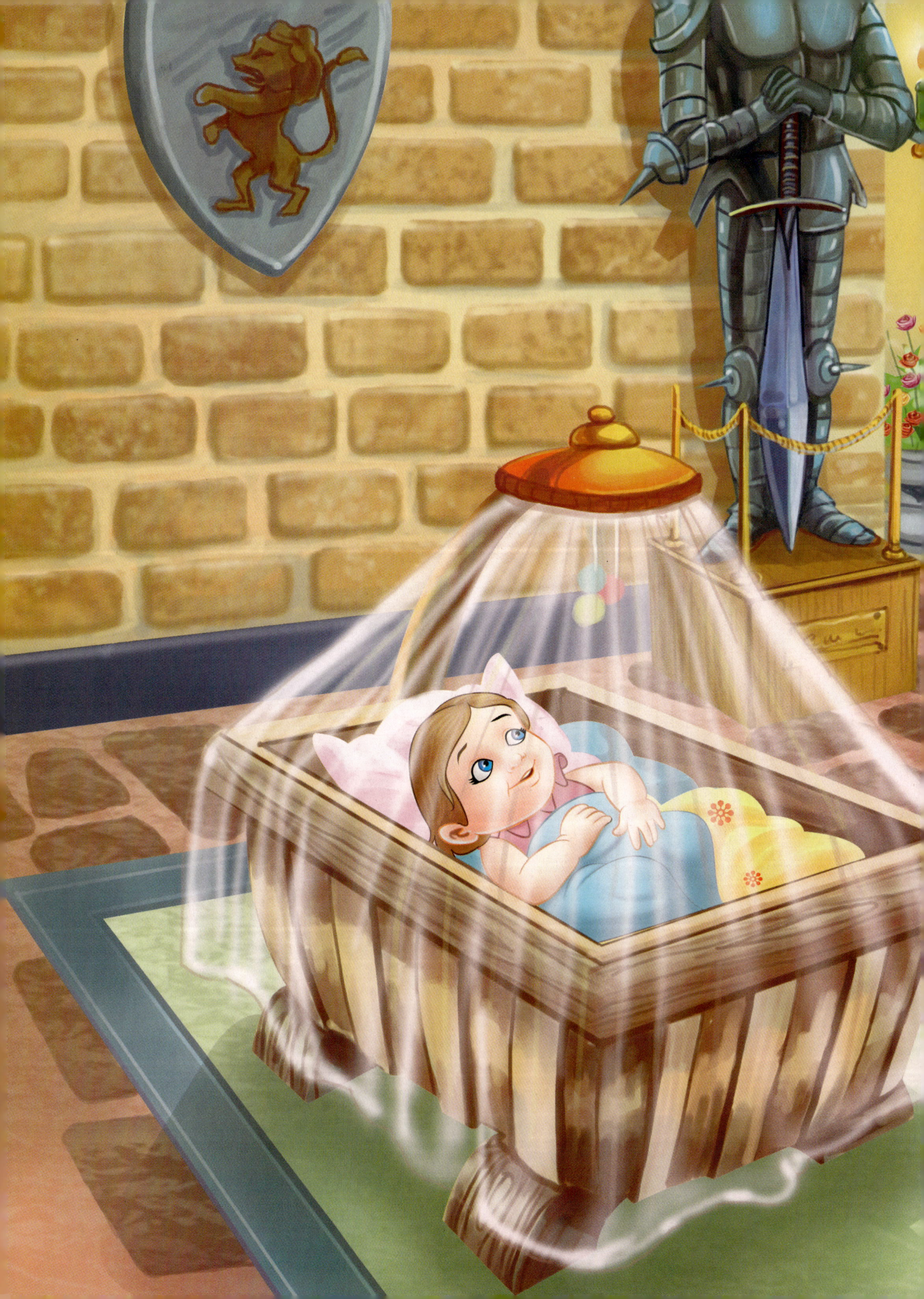

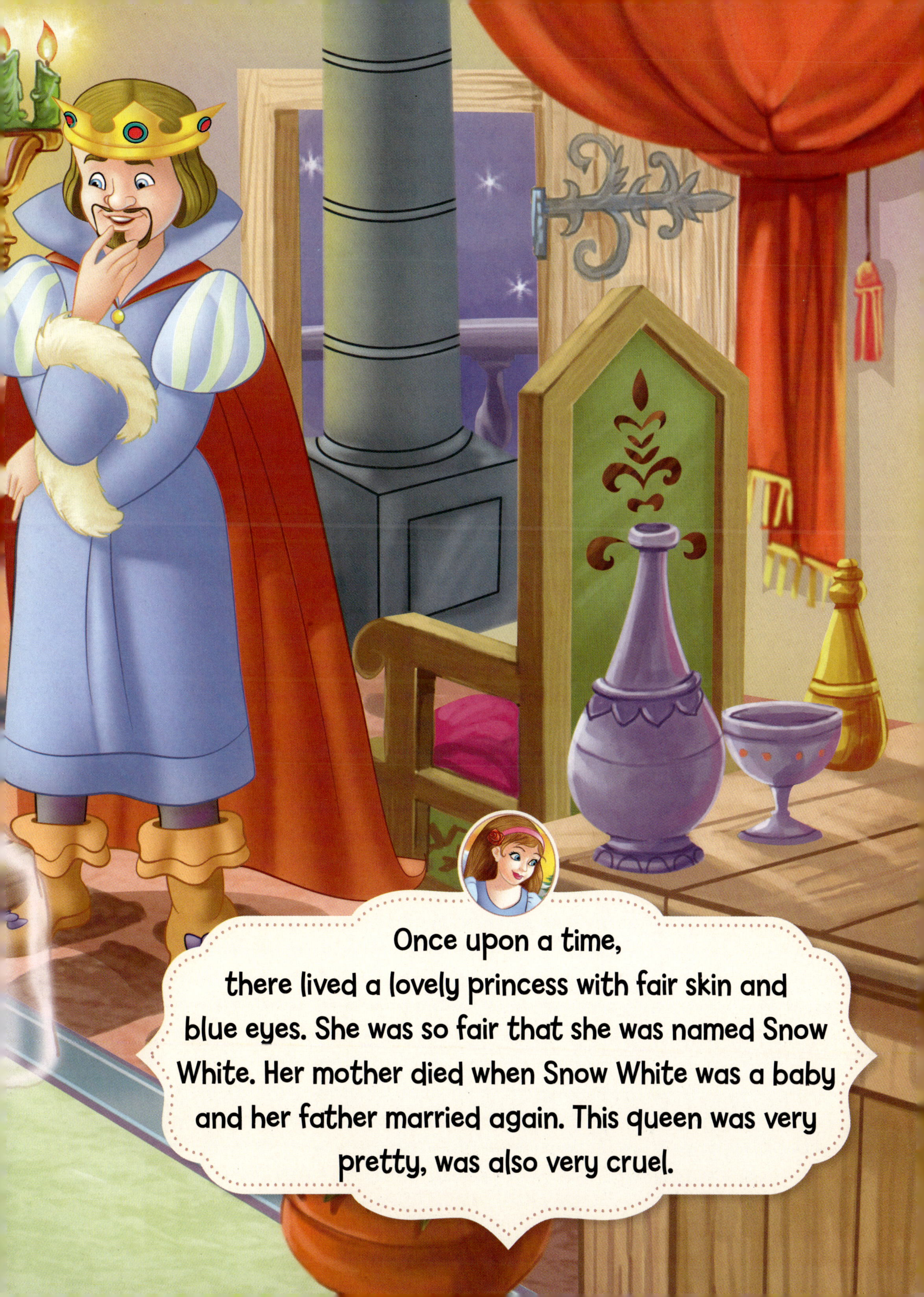

Once upon a time, there lived a lovely princess with fair skin and blue eyes. She was so fair that she was named Snow White. Her mother died when Snow White was a baby and her father married again. This queen was very pretty, was also very cruel.

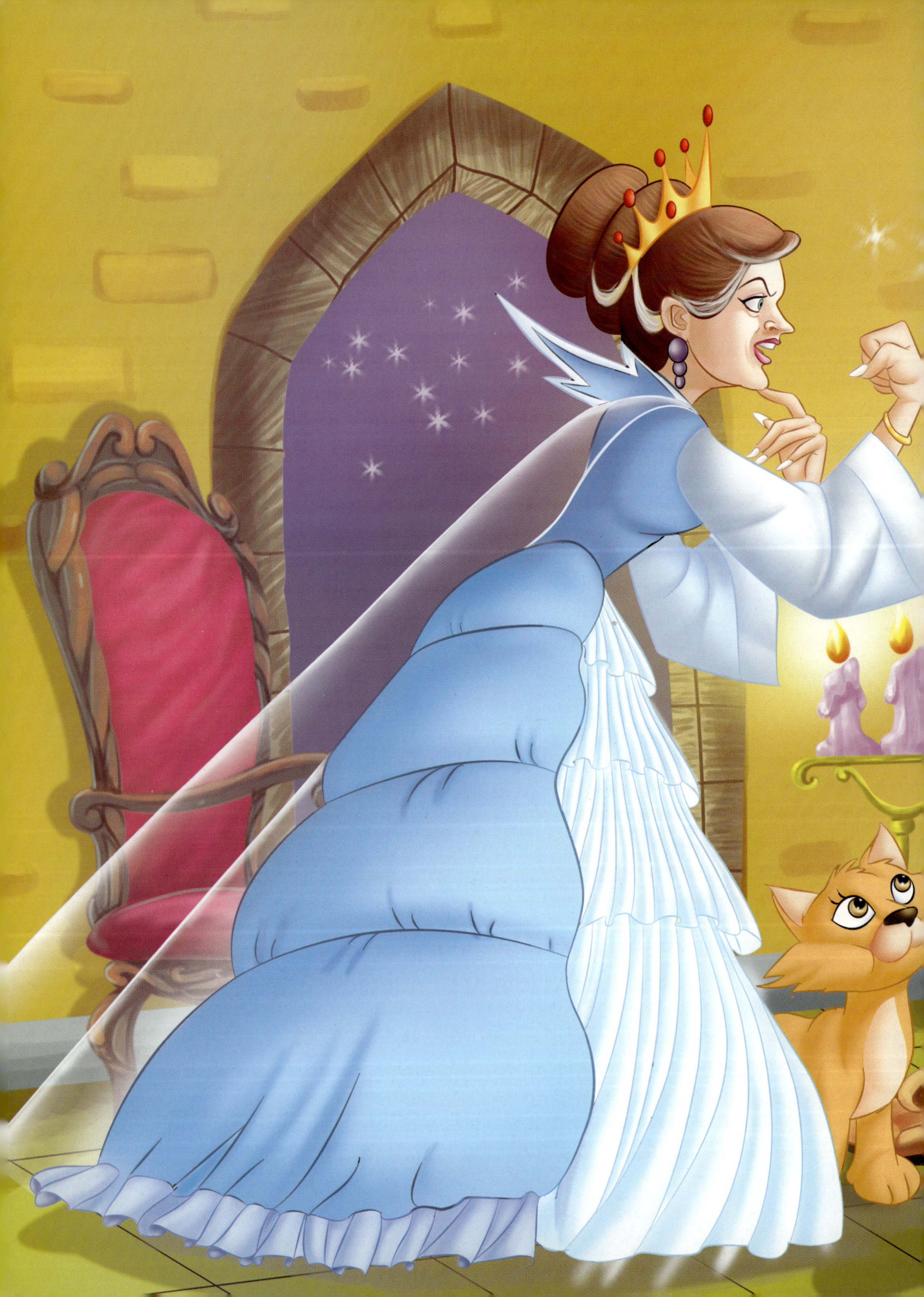

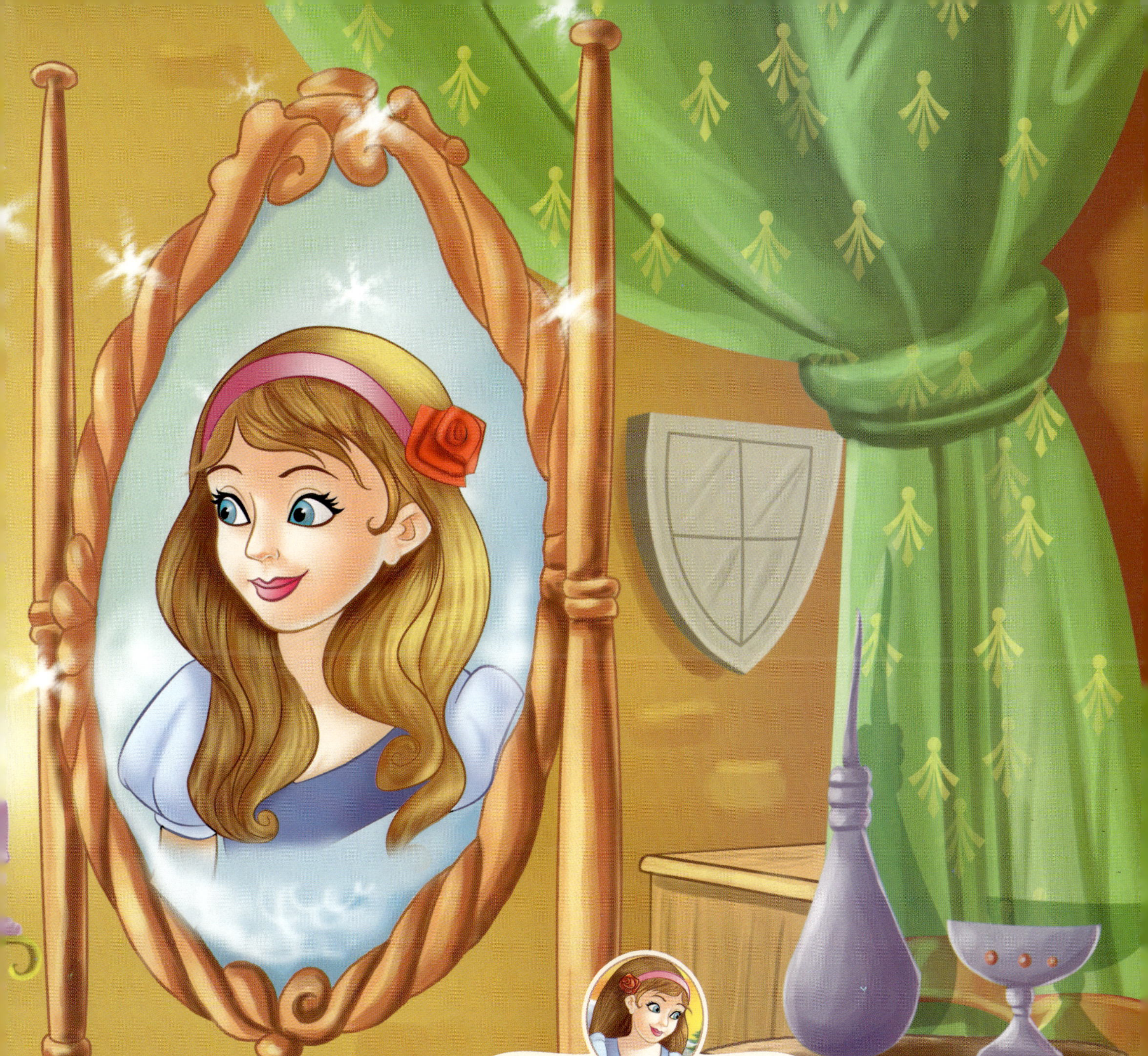

The wicked stepmother wanted to be the most beautiful lady in the kingdom, and she would often ask her magic mirror, “Mirror! Mirror on the wall! Who is the fairest of them all?” And the magic mirror would say, “You are, Your Majesty!” But one day, the mirror replied, “Snow White is the fairest of them all!”

The wicked queen was very angry and jealous of Snow White. She ordered her huntsman to take Snow White to the forest and kill her. "I want you to bring back her heart," she ordered. But when the huntsman reached the forest with Snow White, he took pity on her and set her free.

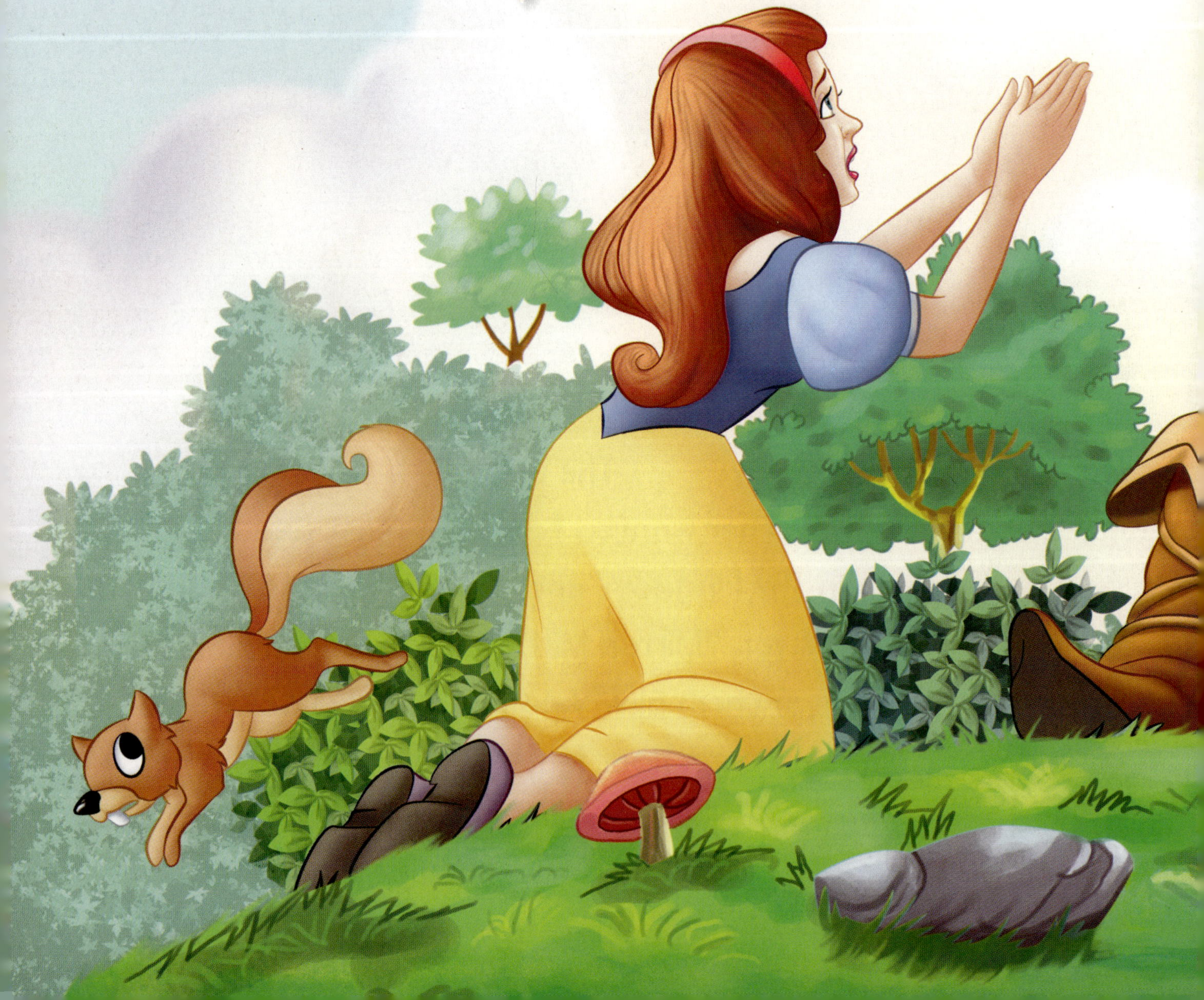

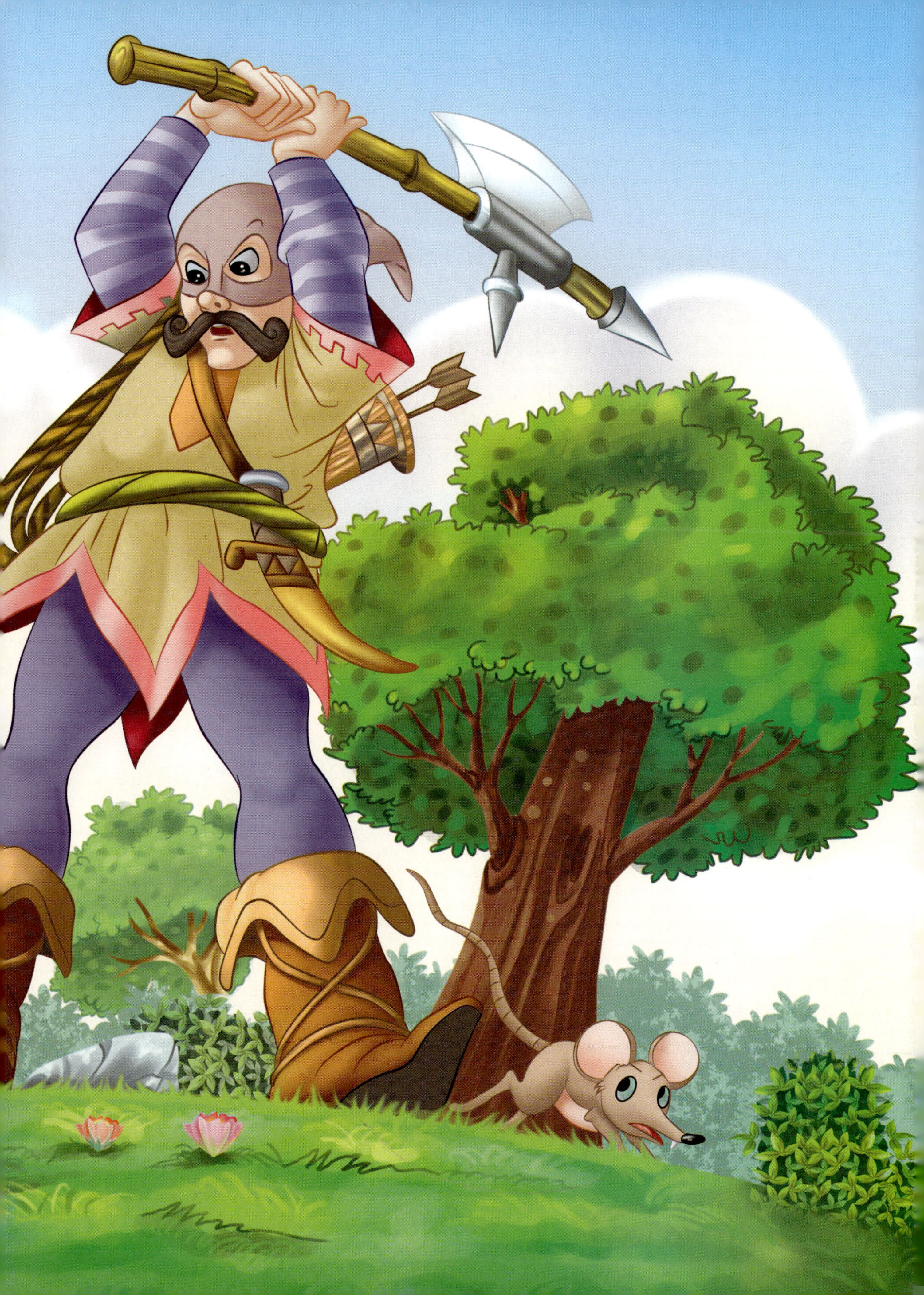

Snow White wandered in the forest all night, crying. When it was daylight, she came to a tiny cottage and went inside. There was nobody there, but she found seven plates on the table and seven tiny beds in the bedroom.

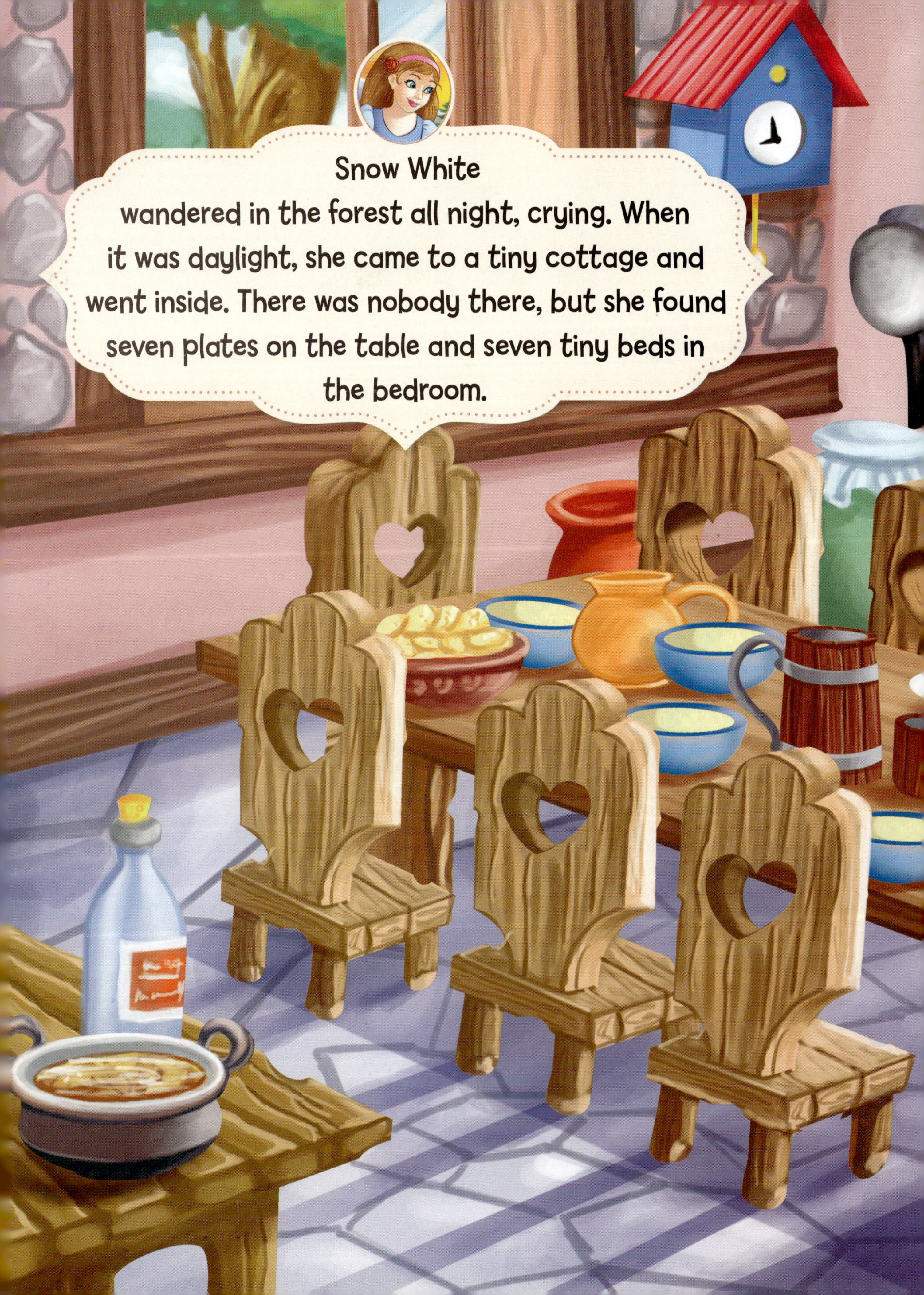

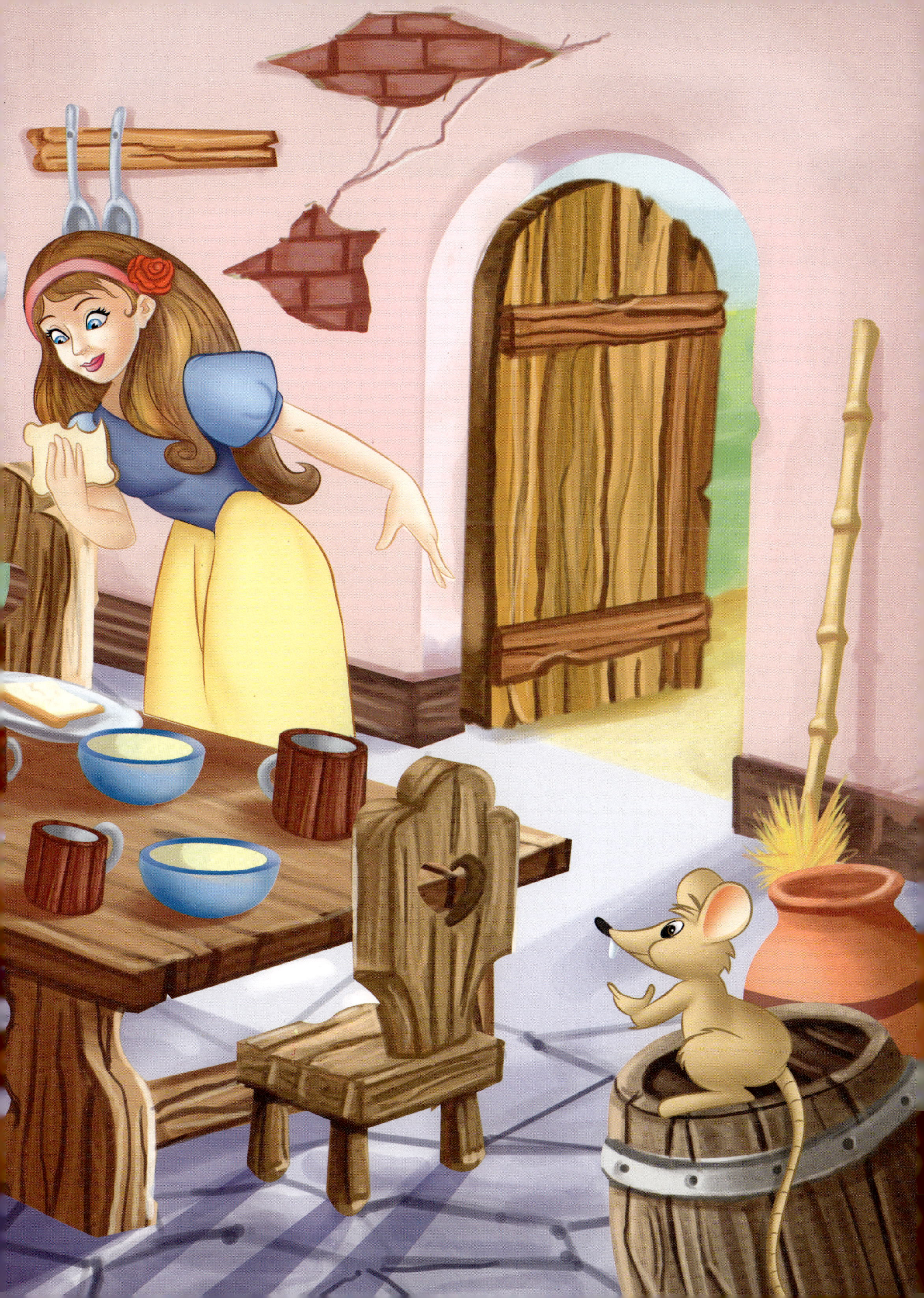

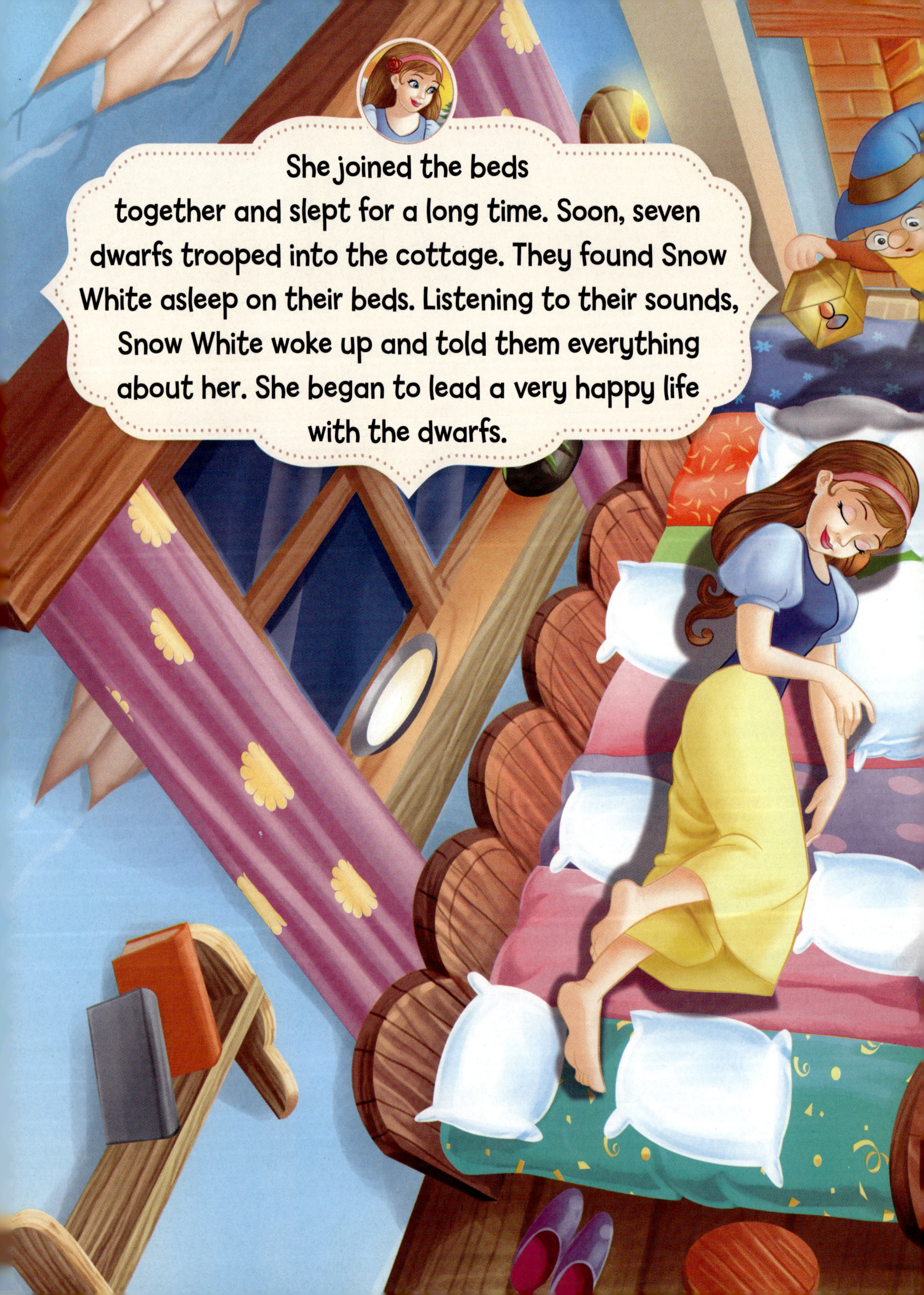

She joined the beds together and slept for a long time. Soon, seven dwarfs trooped into the cottage. They found Snow White asleep on their beds. Listening to their sounds, Snow White woke up and told them everything about her. She began to lead a very happy life with the dwarfs.

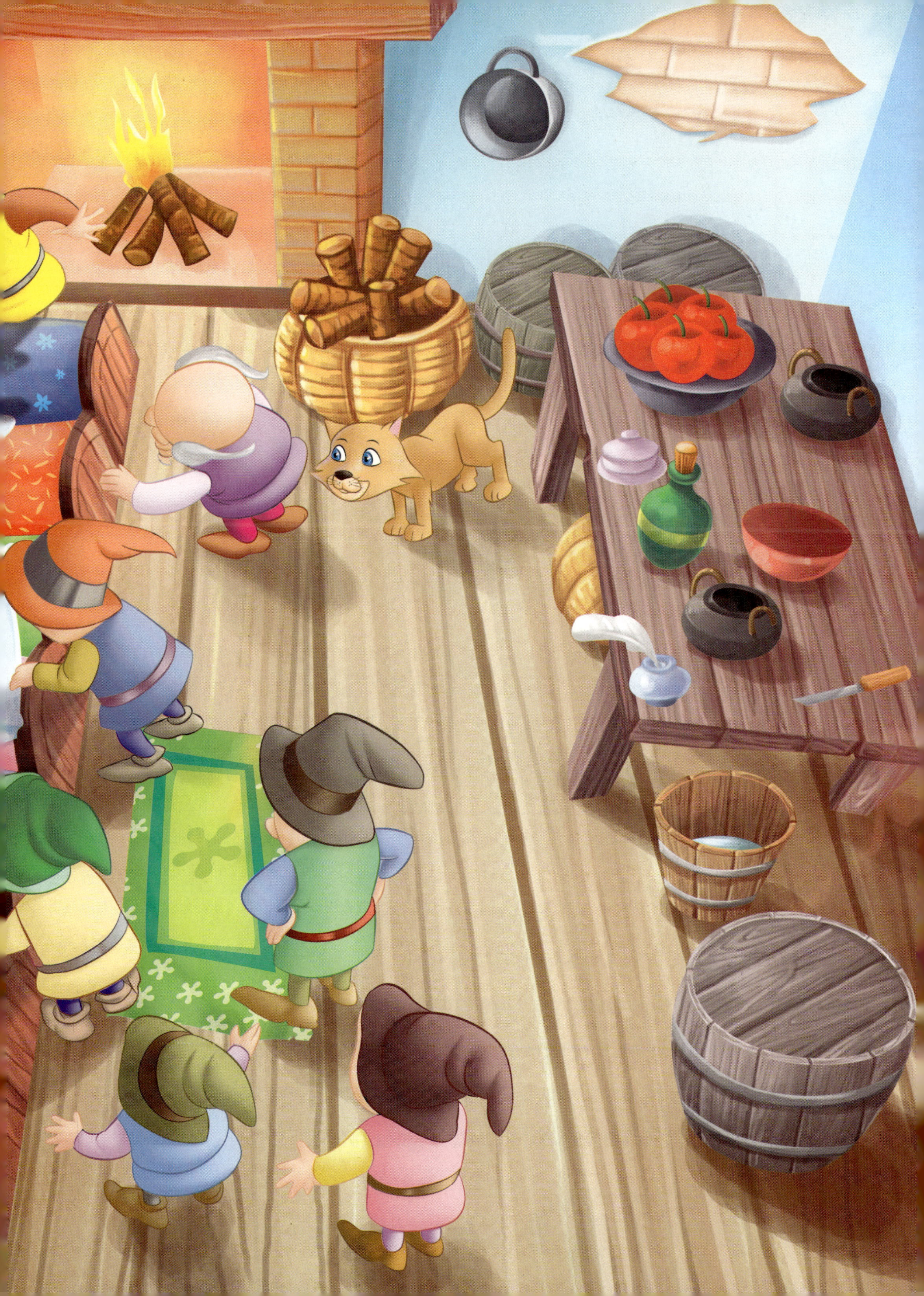

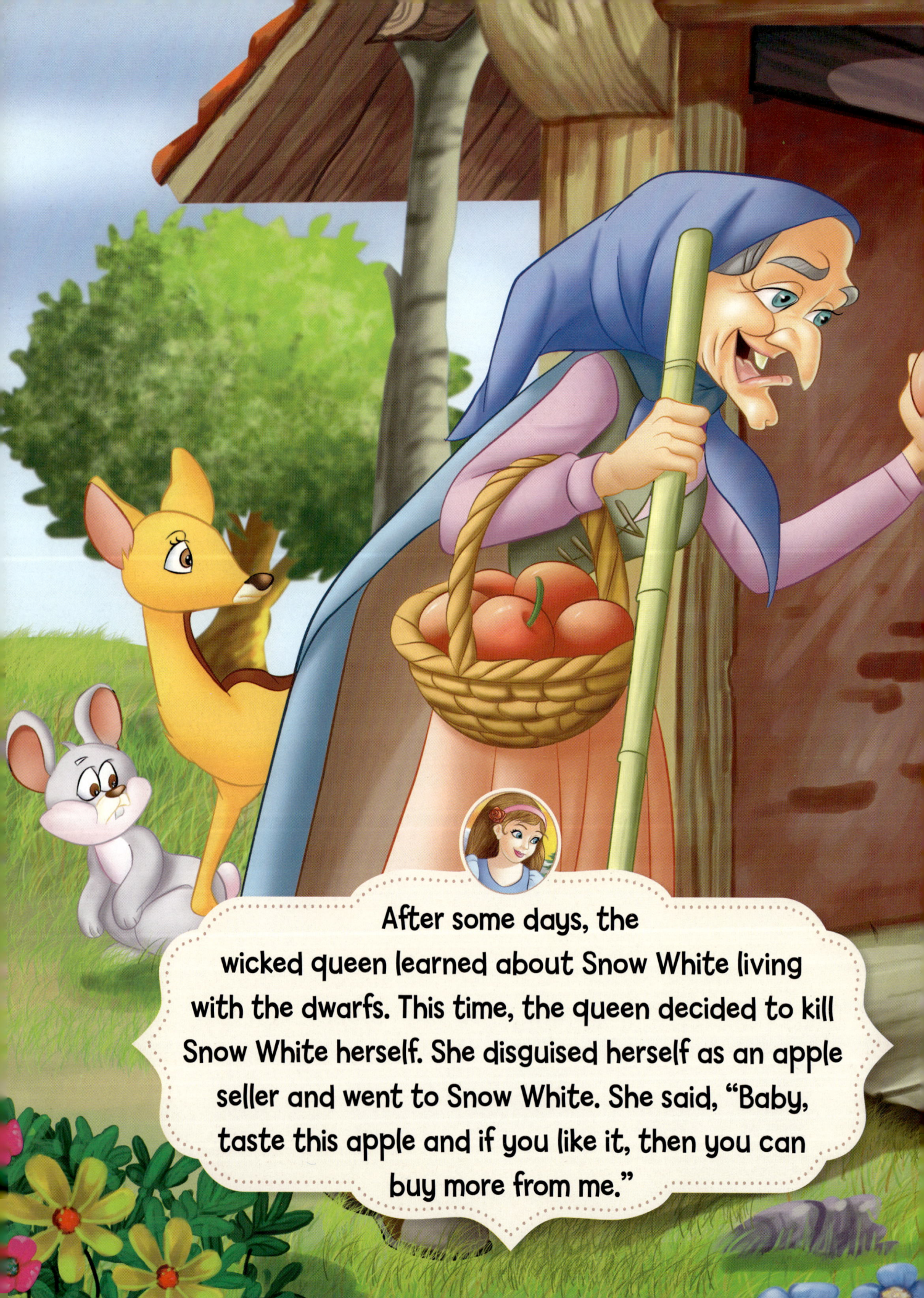

After some days, the wicked queen learned about Snow White living with the dwarfs. This time, the queen decided to kill Snow White herself. She disguised herself as an apple seller and went to Snow White. She said, "Baby, taste this apple and if you like it, then you can buy more from me."

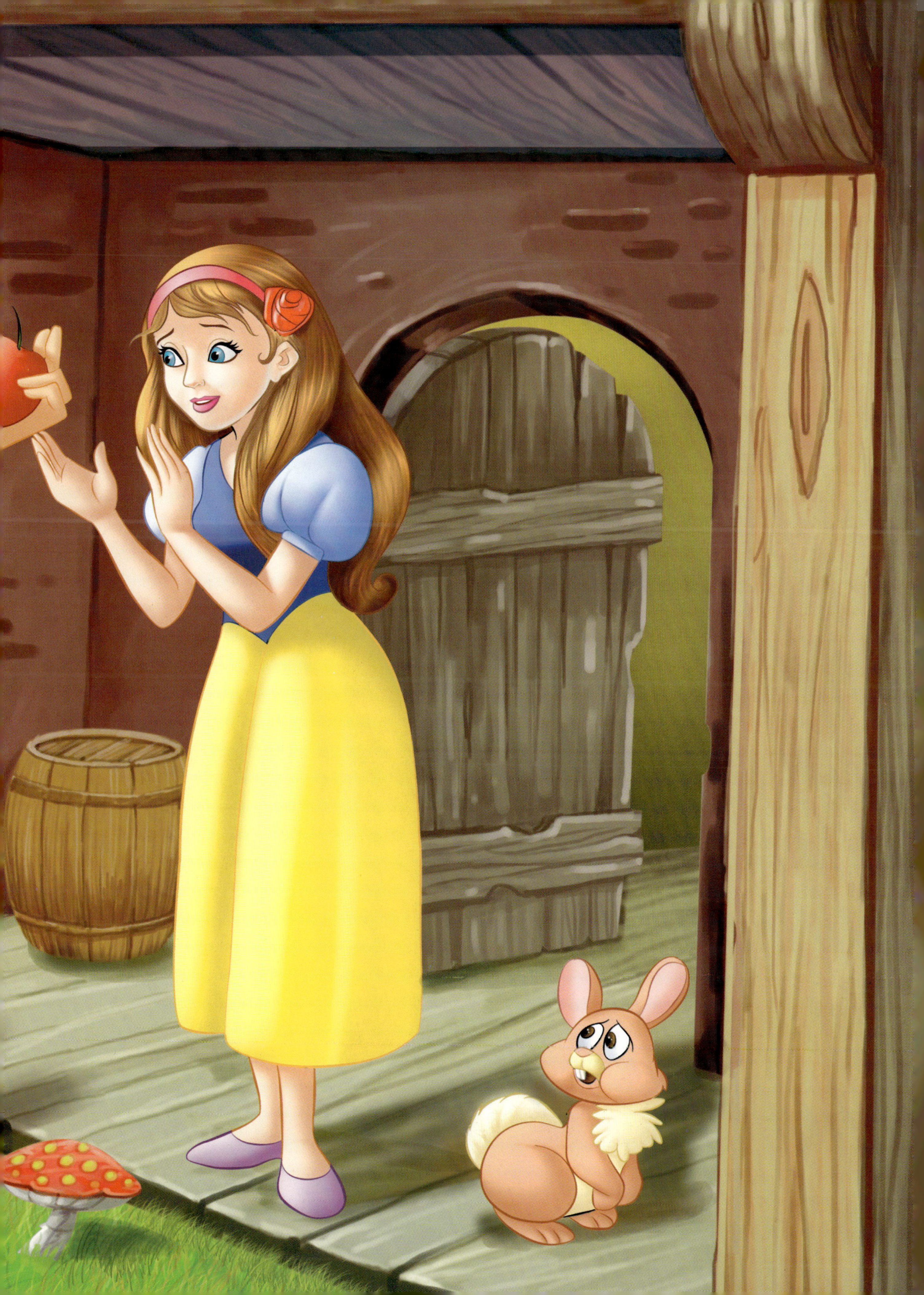

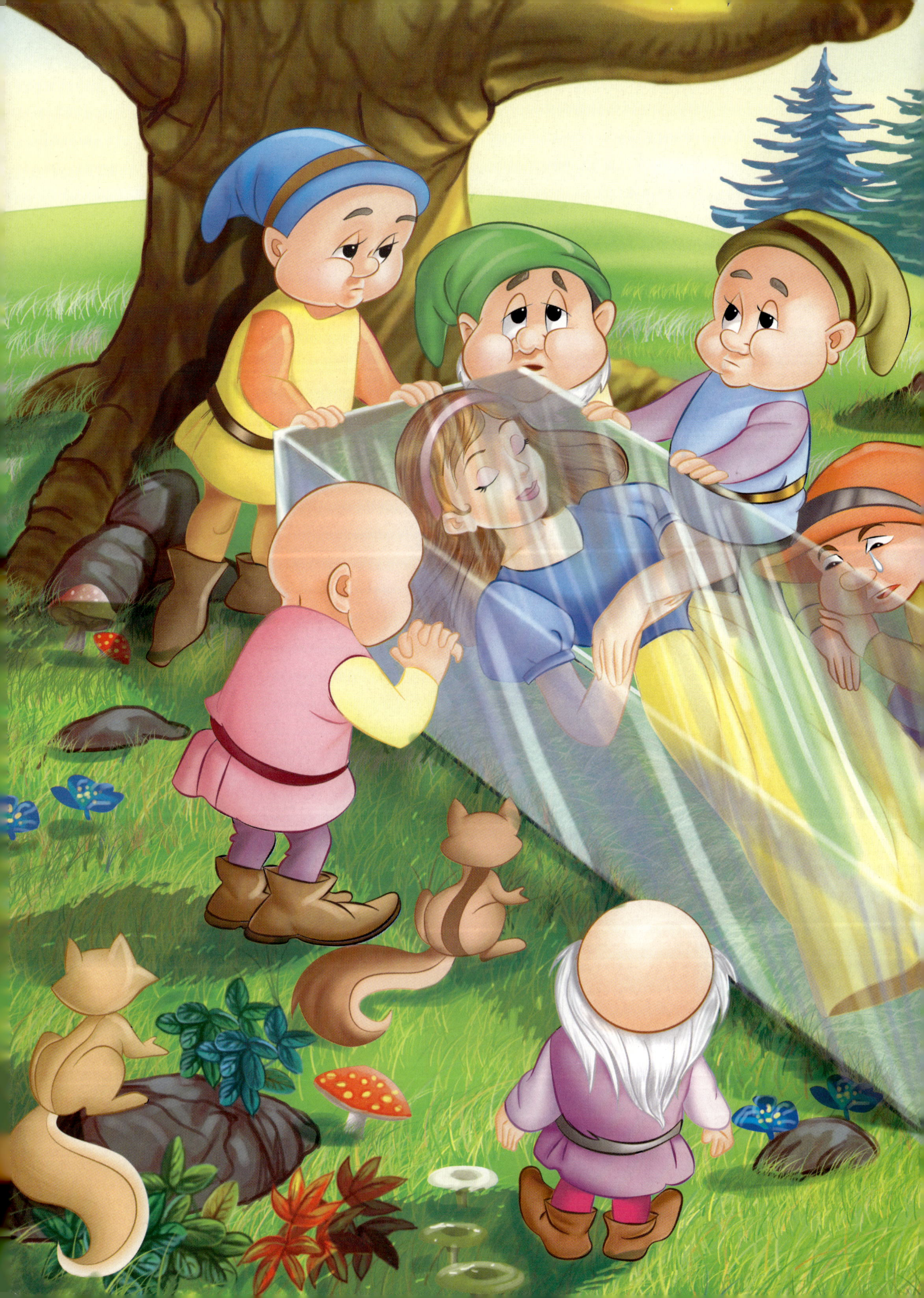

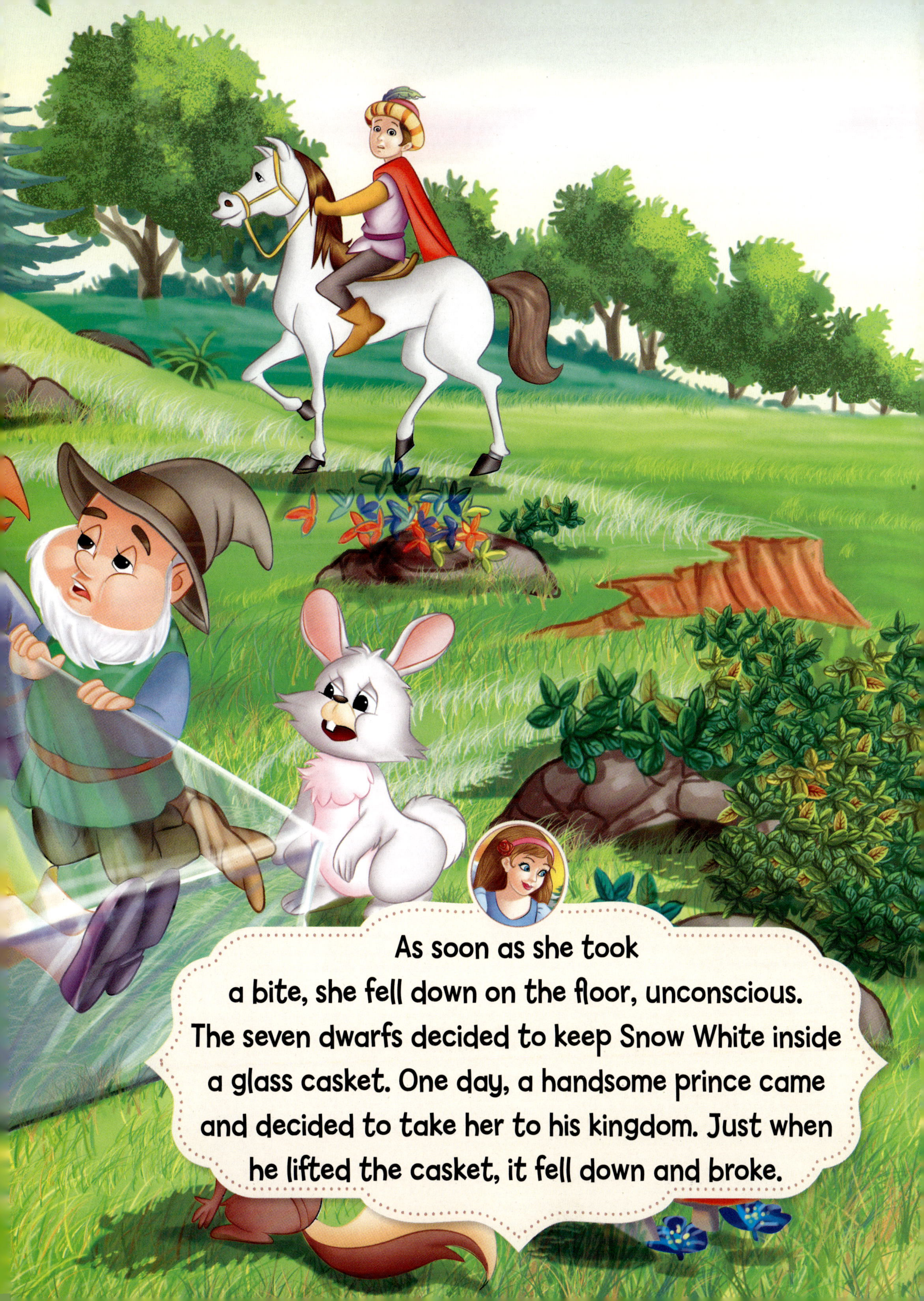

As soon as she took
a bite, she fell down on the floor, unconscious.
The seven dwarfs decided to keep Snow White inside
a glass casket. One day, a handsome prince came
and decided to take her to his kingdom. Just when
he lifted the casket, it fell down and broke.

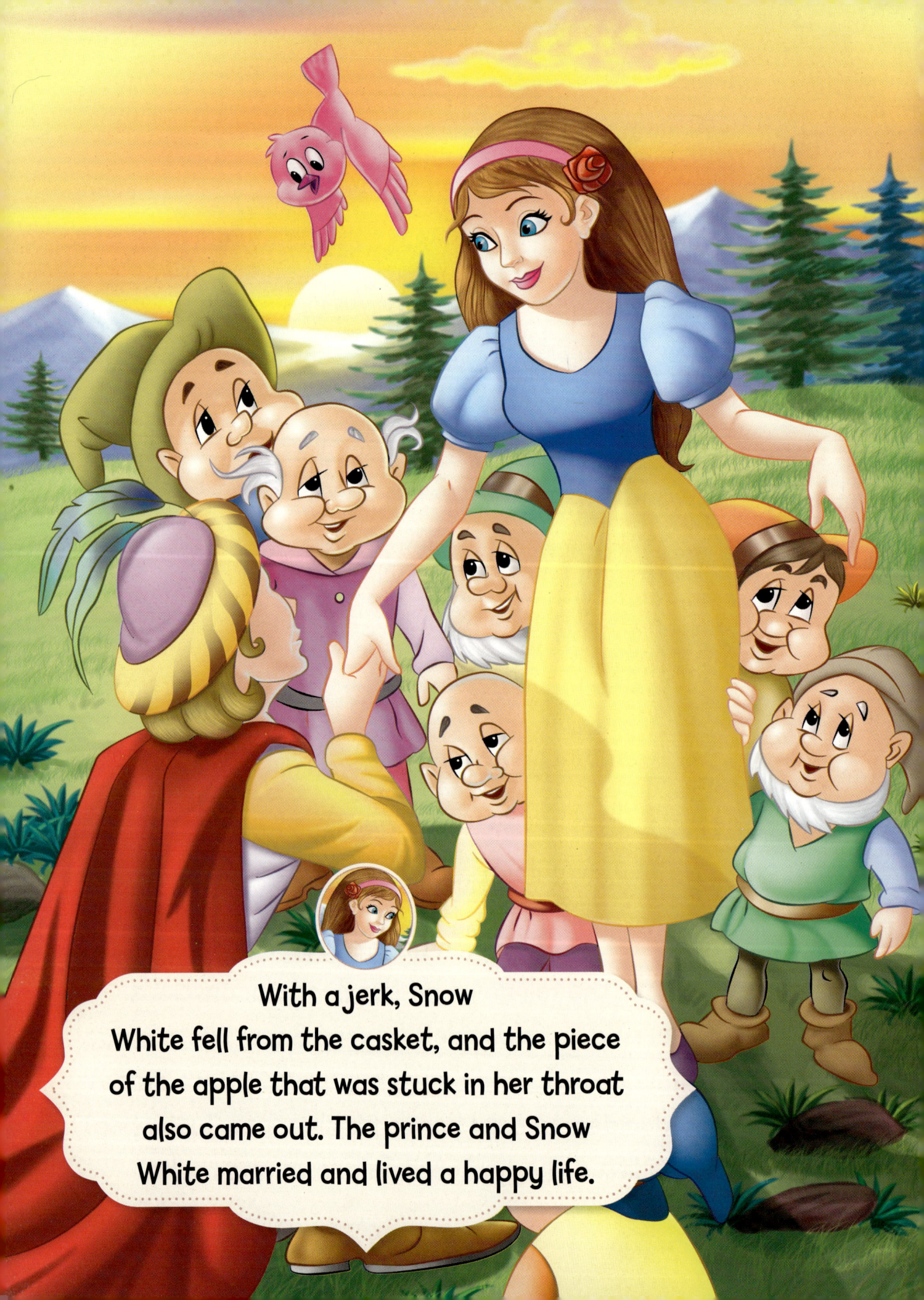

With a jerk, Snow White fell from the casket, and the piece of the apple that was stuck in her throat also came out. The prince and Snow White married and lived a happy life.